Read all the titles in this series

MARY POPE OSBORNE'S

TALES FROM THE

ODYSSEY

Circe's
Island

The
Sirens

Island of
Aeolus

Scylla

Cyclops'
Cave

Island of
the Sun God

Charybdis

Land of the Dead

Calypso's
Island

Land of the
Lotus Eaters

Oceanus

MAP OF ODYSSEUS' JOURNEY

GREECE

Ithaca

Troy

CRETE

T.H. 02

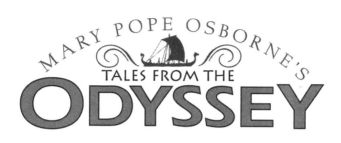

MARY POPE OSBORNE'S

TALES FROM THE

ODYSSEY

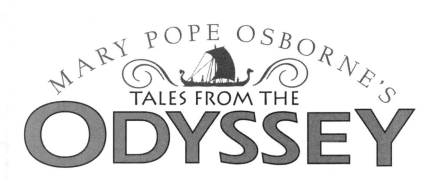

MARY POPE OSBORNE'S
TALES FROM THE
ODYSSEY

Book One

THE ONE-EYED GIANT

By **MARY POPE OSBORNE**
With artwork by **TROY HOWELL**

Hyperion Paperbacks for Children • New York

Special thanks to Frederick J. Booth, Ph.D.,
Professor of Classical Studies, Seton Hall University,
for his expert advice

First Hyperion Paperback edition, 2003

3 5 7 9 10 8 6 4

Printed in the United States of America
Library of Congress Cataloging-in-Publication Data on file.
ISBN 0-7868-0928-0 (pbk.)
Visit www.hyperionchildrensbooks.com

For Wilborn Hampton and LuAnn Walther

CONTENTS

PROLOGUE

$\mathcal{I}$n the early morning of time, there existed a mysterious world called Mount Olympus. Hidden behind a veil of clouds, this world was never swept by winds, nor washed by rains. Those who lived on Mount Olympus never grew old; they never died. They were not humans. They were the mighty gods and goddesses of ancient Greece.

The Olympian gods and goddesses had great power over the lives of the humans who lived on *earth below. Their anger once caused a man named Odysseus to wander the seas for many long years, trying to find his way home.*

Almost three thousand years ago, a Greek poet named Homer first told the story of Odysseus' journey. Since that time, storytellers have told the strange and wondrous tale again and again. We call that story the Odyssey.

THE CALL TO WAR

Long ago on the island of Ithaca in ancient Greece, there lived a man named Odysseus. Though he was king of the island, Odysseus lived a simple life. He enjoyed tending his fields and orchards

and working with his hands as a craftsman and carpenter. More than anything,
he enjoyed the company of his family—
his aged mother and father; his loving
wife, Penelope; and their small son,
Telemachus.

One day as Odysseus was plowing his
fields, he gazed for a long time at Penelope
and Telemachus. The baby was sleeping in
his mother's arms under a nearby tree.
Odysseus imagined that someday he
would teach his son to farm the land and
care for the orchards. He would teach him
to sail a ship around the Greek islands.

As Odysseus dreamed of his son's future, a servant ran from the palace. "A messenger from King Agamemnon has arrived!" the servant shouted.

Dread crept over Odysseus. He knew why the messenger had come. Agamemnon, the ruler of all the Greek islands, was calling for the kings and princes of Greece to wage war against the faraway city of Troy. A Trojan prince had kidnapped a Greek queen named Helen, taking her from her husband.

"Odysseus of Ithaca!" the messenger

shouted. "I bring orders for you to join King Agamemnon in the fight against Troy!"

Odysseus glared at the man, trying desperately to think of some way to avoid leaving his family. Though he was a brave warrior and leader of men, his love for his family overshadowed all else. He loathed the thought of having to leave his home.

"Odysseus!" the messenger shouted. "Remember it was you yourself who first called for our countrymen to swear to defend the marriage of Helen!"

Odysseus remembered this well.

Helen was the most beautiful woman in all the world. When she was old enough to wed, all the princes and kings of Greece had wanted to marry her. Fearing that the men's jealousies would bring their nation to ruin, Odysseus had urged them all to swear to defend Helen's marriage always, no matter who she chose for her husband.

"In the name of Agamemnon, I command you to set sail at once!" the man shouted.

Ignoring the messenger, Odysseus began to behave in a strange way. Instead of yoking two oxen together to pull his plow, he yoked an ox to a small donkey. Instead of casting seeds into the furrows of his fields, he cast salt. He hoped the messenger would think he had gone mad.

But the messenger suspected Odysseus was only pretending. To test him, the messenger snatched Telemachus from Penelope's arms and placed the baby in front of Odysseus' plow.

Penelope screamed.

Odysseus quickly turned his plow so he would not harm the boy. And in that moment, he knew he had sealed his fate. He had proved his sanity. He would now have to leave his family and answer the call to war.

THE WOODEN HORSE

*F*or the next ten years, Odysseus camped with a thousand Greek warriors outside the walls of Troy. He despaired that the war would ever end. The Greeks slew many Trojan leaders in battle, including the prince who had stolen Helen from her Greek husband. But Helen herself remained captive within the thick walls of Troy. The Greeks had not been able to find a way to enter the city and take her back.

One day, Odysseus left the Greek camp and sat alone on the Trojan shore. He mourned the separation from his wife and felt terribly sad that he had missed seeing his son grow up. He feared that his mother and father might have died while he was at war, and that he would never lay eyes on them again.

Suddenly, a tall woman appeared before Odysseus. She wore a shining helmet and carried a spear and shield. The woman was Athena, the goddess of wisdom and war and a daughter of Zeus.

Athena stared at Odysseus with flashing gray eyes. Though her gaze was fierce, it was also kind. Athena had always been fond of Odysseus. She admired his skills as a carpenter and craftsman. And she loved him for his strength and clever ways.

Odysseus was speechless as he stood before the goddess.

"I have come to help you take Helen back from the Trojans," she said. "Here is how you shall bring down the walls of Troy. Direct your carpenters to build a giant wooden horse. Hide with a few of your men inside the horse while the rest of the Greeks pretend to leave the island in defeat. Thinking the horse has been abandoned, the Trojans will bring it inside their walls. When night falls and the Greek soldiers return, open the gates of the city and let them in."

The goddess then left as quickly as she had come.

Odysseus set to work at once. He called for his best carpenter and directed him to build the giant wooden horse. When the horse was finished, Odysseus ordered his men to carve Athena's name into its side. He then chose his bravest warriors and led them up a rope ladder to a secret trapdoor in the belly of the horse. He and his men locked themselves inside and waited.

Soon Odysseus heard the Greek warriors set fire to their camp. He heard them board their ships and sail away in the night.

Odysseus dared not sleep as he waited

for morning. After many hours, he heard seagulls crying in the dawn light. Then he heard footsteps on the sand and voices.

"What is this horse?" a Trojan shouted. "Why did the Greeks build it, and then abandon it on our shore?"

"It is ours now!" said another. "Let us haul it inside our walls!"

"No, we must not!" cried another. "We must never trust gifts from the Greeks! Throw this monstrous thing into the sea!"

"Burn it!" some yelled.

"Let it stay!" others shouted.

The argument was interrupted by a

Greek soldier who had stayed behind and allowed himself to be captured by the Trojans. Now he claimed to be a traitor to the Greeks.

"This horse is a gift for Athena," he lied. "See her name carved into its side? If you destroy it, the goddess will punish you. But if you give it a place of honor in your city, she will give Troy power over all the world."

The Trojans argued bitterly about whether or not to trust the captive. Finally, the king made a decision. "We will keep the wooden horse," he said.

"Bring it inside the gates of Troy."

Odysseus felt great relief and excitement. Athena's plan was working! He and his men scarcely breathed as the Trojans heaved the giant horse onto rollers, then pushed it into the city.

Odysseus waited patiently for night to come. When all was silent, he opened the trapdoor in the horse's belly.

It was pitch-black outside. The city was eerily calm. All the Trojans had returned to their homes and gone to bed.

Under the cover of darkness, Odysseus led the way down the rope ladder. He and his men crept to the city gates, unbolted them, and threw them open.

Hordes of Greek warriors were waiting on the other side! In the darkness, they had sailed back to Troy and silently gathered outside the gates.

With a horrifying battle cry, the Greek army rushed into the city. They killed many men and captured women and children to keep as slaves. They found Helen and returned her to her Greek husband.

By dawn, the entire city of Troy was in flames. The triumphant Greek warriors loaded their ships with treasure. Then finally, after ten long years, they set sail for home.

As a strong wind carried Odysseus and his twelve sleek ships away from the shores of Troy, he was jubilant. He imagined all of Ithaca rejoicing over his victorious return. He imagined himself soon embracing his beloved wife and son, and his parents. Never had he felt so hopeful and happy.

THE ODYSSEY BEGINS

$\mathcal{S}$oon after the Greek ships left Troy, the skies began to blacken. Lightning zig-zagged above the foamy sea. Thunder shook the heavens.

Mighty winds stirred the water. The

waves grew higher and higher, until they were rolling over the bows of the ships.

"The gods are punishing us!" the Greek warriors shouted. "We shall all drown!"

As his men frantically fought the storm, Odysseus felt bewildered. Why was Zeus, god of the skies, hurling his thunderbolts at them? Why was Poseidon, lord of the seas, sending great waves over the waters?

Odysseus turned to his men. "What has happened to anger the gods?" he shouted. "Tell me!"

"Before we left Troy, Greek warriors invaded Athena's temple!" said one of his men. "They were violent and disrespectful."

Odysseus was stunned. The Greeks had offended the goddess who had helped them to victory! And now her anger might drown them all.

The wind grew stronger. It whipped the sails of the Greek ships and slashed them to rags. "Lift your oars!" Odysseus shouted to his men. "Row! Row to shore!"

The Greeks struggled valiantly against the mighty wind and waves. Fighting for their lives, they finally rowed their battered ships to a strange shore. There they found shelter in a rocky cave.

The storm raged for two more days and nights. Then, on the third day, a fair wind blew, the sun came out, and the wine-dark sea was calm at last.

"Now we can continue on our way," Odysseus said to his men. "Athena is no longer angry." In the rosy dawn, he ordered them to raise their tattered sails and set off again for Ithaca.

But, alas, the wrath of Athena had not been fully spent. Hardly had Odysseus reached the open sea than another gale began to blow.

For many days, Odysseus and his men fought the wind and the waves, refusing to surrender to the storm. Finally, on the tenth day, there was sudden calm.

Odysseus ordered his fleet to sail into the cove of a leafy green island. There he hoped to find food and drink for his hungry, weary men.

The Greeks dropped anchor. Then they dragged themselves ashore. They drank cool, fresh water from a spring and collapsed onto the sand.

As Odysseus rested, he ordered three of his men to explore the island and look for provisions.

When the three had not returned by late afternoon, Odysseus grew angry. Why did they tarry? he wondered.

Odysseus set out in search of the men. He moved through the brush and brambles, calling their names.

He had not gone far when he came upon a group of peaceful islanders. They greeted him with warm, friendly smiles. And they offered him their food—lovely bright flowers.

Odysseus was famished. But just as he was about to eat the flowers, he caught sight of his missing men. The three were lying on the ground with dreamy smiles on their faces.

Odysseus called each man by name, but none of them answered. They did not even look at him.

"What have you done to them?" he asked the islanders.

"We have given them our flowers to eat," an islander answered. "This is our greatest gift. The gods would be angry if we did not offer to feed our guests."

"What sort of flowers are these?" Odysseus asked.

"They come from the lotus tree," the islander said. "They have the magical power of forgetfulness. They make a man forget the past."

"Forget his memories of home?" asked Odysseus. "And his memories of his family and friends?"

The lotus-eaters only smiled. They again offered Odysseus their sweet, lovely flowers. But he roughly brushed them away. He pulled his three men to their feet and commanded them all to return to their ships at once.

The men began to weep. They begged to be left behind so they could stay on the island and eat lotus flowers forever.

Odysseus angrily herded the men back to the ships. As they drew near the shore, the three tried to escape. Odysseus called for help.

"Tie their hands and feet!" he shouted to his crew. "Make haste! Before others eat the magic flowers and forget their homes, too!"

The three flailing men were hauled aboard and tied to rowing benches. Then

Odysseus ordered the twelve ships to push off from shore.

Once more, the Greeks set sail for Ithaca, sweeping the gray sea with their long oars. As they rowed past dark islands with jagged rocks and shadowy coves, Odysseus felt troubled and anxious. What other strange wonders lurked on these dark, unknown shores?

FOUR

THE MYSTERIOUS SHORE

Soon the Greek ships came upon a hilly island, thick with trees. No humans seemed to live there. Hundreds of wild goats could be heard bleating from the island's gloomy thickets.

Odysseus ordered his men to drop anchor in the shelter of a mist-covered bay. By the time the Greeks had lowered their sails, night had fallen. The moon was hidden by clouds. In the pitch dark, the men lay down on the sandy shore and slept.

When daylight came, the men woke to see woodland nymphs, the daughters of Zeus, driving wild goats down from the hills. The hungry Greeks eagerly grabbed their bows and spears and slew more than a hundred goats.

All day, the Greeks lingered on the island, feasting on roasted meat and drinking sweet wine. As the sun went down, they stared at a mysterious shore across the water. Smoke rose from fires on the side of a mountain. The murmur of deep voices and the bleating of sheep wafted through the twilight.

Who lives there? Who stokes those fires? Odysseus wondered silently. *Are they friendly or lawless men?*

Darkness fell, and the Greeks slept once more on the sand. When he was wakened by the rosy dawn, Odysseus stared again at the mysterious shore in the distance. Though he was yearning to set sail for

Ithaca, a strange curiosity had taken hold of him.

Odysseus woke his men. "I must know who lives on that far shore," he said. "With a single ship, I will lead an expedition to find out whether they are savages or civilized humans. Then we will continue our journey home."

Odysseus chose his bravest men to go with him. They untied a ship from their fleet and pushed off from the island.

Soon the Greeks were swinging their long oars into the calm face of the sea, rowing toward the mysterious shore.

When they drew close, they dropped anchor beneath a tall, rocky cliff.

Odysseus filled a goatskin with the best wine he had on board, made from the sweetest grapes. "This will be our gift to repay the hospitality of anyone who welcomes us into his home," he said.

He ordered some of his men to remain with the ship, then led the rest up the side of the cliff. On a ledge high above the water, they discovered a large, shady clearing. On the other side of the clearing, creeping vines hung over the mouth of a cave. The Greeks pushed past the vines and stepped inside.

The cave was filled with young goats and lambs. Pots of cheese and pails of goat's milk were everywhere. But there was no sign of a shepherd.

"Hurry!" said one of Odysseus' men. "Let us grab provisions and leave!"

"Yes! We should drive the lambs down to our ship before their master returns!" said another.

"No," said Odysseus. "We will wait awhile. . . . I am curious to see who lives here."

The Greeks made a fire and gave an

offering to the gods. Then they greedily took their fill of milk and cheese. Finally, in the late afternoon, they heard whistling and bleating.

"Ah, the shepherd returns," Odysseus said. "Let us step forward and meet this man."

But when they peered out of the cave, the Greeks gasped with horror—for the shepherd was not a man at all. He was a monster.

THE ONE-EYED GIANT

A hideous giant lumbered into the clearing. He carried nearly half a forest's worth of wood on his back. His monstrous head jutted from his body like a shaggy mountain peak. A single eye bulged in the center of his forehead.

The monster was Polyphemus. He was the most savage of all the Cyclopes, a race of fierce one-eyed giants who lived without laws or leaders. The Cyclopes were ruthless creatures who were known to capture and devour any sailors who happened near their shores.

Polyphemus threw down his pile of wood. As it crashed to the ground, Odysseus and his men fled to the darkest corners of the cave.

Unaware that the Greeks were hiding inside, Polyphemus drove his animals into the cave. Then he rolled a huge boulder over its mouth to block out the light of day and imprison his flock inside.

Twenty-four wagons could not haul that rock away, Odysseus thought desperately. *How will we escape this monster?*

Odysseus' men trembled with terror as the giant made a small fire and milked his goats in the shadowy light. His milking done, he threw more wood on his fire. The flame blazed brightly, lighting up the corners of the cave where Odysseus and his men were hiding.

"What's this? Who are you? From

where do you come?" the giant boomed. He glared at the Greeks with his single eye. "Are you pirates who steal the treasure of others?"

Odysseus' men were frozen with terror. But Odysseus hid his own fear and stepped toward the monster.

"We are not pirates," he said. "We are Greeks blown off course by storm winds. Will you offer us the gift of hospitality like a good host? If you do, mighty Zeus, king of the gods, will be pleased. Zeus is the guardian of all strangers."

"Fool!" the giant growled. "Who are

you to tell me to please Zeus? I am a son of Poseidon, god of the seas! I am not afraid of Zeus!"

Odysseus' men cowered in fear.

Polyphemus moved closer to Odysseus. He spoke in a soft, terrible voice. "But tell me, stranger, where is your ship? Near or far from shore?"

Odysseus knew Polyphemus was try- ing to trap him. "Our ship was destroyed in the storm," he lied. "It was dashed against the rocks. With these good men, I escaped. I ask you again, will you welcome us?"

The Cyclops stared for a moment at Odysseus. Then, without warning, he grabbed two Greeks. He smashed them against the stone floor, killing them at once. The giant tore the men limb from limb and devoured them—flesh, bones, and all.

The rest of Odysseus' men cried aloud with horror. They raised their arms to Mount Olympus, begging Zeus for help. Odysseus gathered his strength and commanded his men to be silent.

The giant washed down his gruesome

meal with a bucket of goat's milk. "There!" he said, smacking his lips. "Let that be my welcome to you."

The monster belched. Then he lay down on the floor among his fat sheep and tiny lambs. Soon he was fast asleep and snoring.

Trembling with rage, Odysseus drew his sword, ready to slay the bloodthirsty beast. But wisdom stopped him.

He took a deep breath. "We can never roll that rock away from the entrance," he said to his horror-stricken men. "If I slay the brute, we will die, too, trapped forever in his wretched lair."

Odysseus put away his weapon. He had no choice but to wait for morning— and for the giant to wake.

SIX

ODYSSEUS' PLAN

*A*fter many terrible hours, the light of dawn crept through the cracks at the mouth of the cave.

Odysseus watched the Cyclops open his eye, then heave himself up from the ground. The giant lit a fire and milked his goats. When he was done with his chores, he snatched up two more Greeks.

The terrified warriors again begged for Zeus to help them. But as before, the mighty god did not heed their cries.

Odysseus and his men watched the monster smash their two comrades against a stone wall, then devour them for breakfast.

The Greeks reeled at the horror of the sight. Again, Odysseus felt a murderous rage toward the monster, but again he fought to conceal it.

After his gory meal, Polyphemus rolled away the boulder from the mouth of the cave. He called for his flock and led them out into the sunlight. Then he rolled the mighty rock back against the entrance, trapping the Greeks inside. They could hear the monster whistling as he drove his goats and sheep down the mountain slope.

Odysseus and his men were sickened by the gruesome murder of their friends. The men moaned and wept, but Odysseus ordered them to be silent.

"Weeping will not save us," he said. "We must make a plan."

His men were too distraught to think clearly, so Odysseus paced about the cave alone, searching for a way to destroy the giant.

Peering about the shadowy cave, Odysseus caught sight of the giant's club. Made from fresh green olive wood, the club was as tall as the mast of a twenty-oared trading ship.

Odysseus seized the club and chopped off a six-foot stake. He ordered his men to carve the wood into a spike. When they were done, he honed one end until it was razor sharp.

"Now, let us draw lots to see who will help me," he said.

The men drew lots, and four were chosen to help. Odysseus told them his plan. Then he hid the stake in the shadows of the cave.

"All we can do now is wait," he said.

His men huddled together like frightened children. But as Odysseus sat and stared at the entrance of the cave, his heart grew cold and hard.

Finally, he heard the awful whistling of the monster, then the bleating of sheep.

The huge rock was rolled away. Sunlight streamed into the cave. Flocks of sheep and goats bounded in. The one-eyed giant lumbered behind them.

Once all were inside, Polyphemus again rolled the boulder against the mouth of the cave. Without even a glance at the Greeks, he stoked his fires and set about milking his goats.

The Cyclops finished his chores. Then just as suddenly as before, he grabbed two more men. He bashed them against the stone floor and ate them for supper. When he had finished his meal of flesh and bone, the one-eyed giant grinned horribly at the remaining Greeks.

Odysseus' men cried out in terror before the bloody monster.

Odysseus himself trembled with fury. But he forced himself to smile. He rose calmly and picked up his wineskin. With a steady hand, he poured sweet red wine into a wooden bowl.

"Here, sir," he said, offering the bowl to the Cyclops. "Please drink our good wine. I give it to you as a gift with the hope that you will take pity on us and help us find our way home."

The giant snatched the bowl from Odysseus and gulped down the wine.

When he was done, he held out the bowl and thundered, "MORE! MORE! Give me MORE!"

Odysseus poured more wine into the bowl, and Polyphemus gulped it all down.

"MORE!" the monster bellowed. "MORE! And tell me your name!"

Odysseus filled the bowl a third time. The giant poured it down his throat. Then he put down the bowl and began to stagger about the cave. Odysseus saw that the wine had gone to the giant's head. He knew it would soon be time to act.

"Sir, you have asked me for my name,"

said Odysseus. "I will give it to you as a gift. But you must give me a gift in return. My name is No One. That is what everyone calls me. No One."

The giant laughed cruelly.

"Ha! No One!" he said. "Thank you for your gift. Now I give you a gift in return. It is this: I will eat you and all of your men. But I will eat you last! That is my gift to you, No One. Ha-ha-ha!"

As he laughed, the giant lost his balance. He staggered back a few steps. Then he slid down the stone wall and crashed to the ground. His huge head drooped to one side. His eye closed and he began to snore. The giant's snores were so thunderous that all the milk pails rattled throughout the cave.

Odysseus moved quickly. He jammed the sharpened end of the stake into the burning embers. He beckoned to his men to stand near him. Then he pulled the stake from the fire.

"Help us, O Zeus!" Odysseus prayed.

The mighty god finally seemed to hear his prayer. As Odysseus took a deep breath, he felt a surge of strength and power.

Odysseus gave a sign. Then all together,

the men raised the stake and rammed its burning point into the giant's huge, bulging eye.

The Cyclops let out a piercing howl.

The eye hissed and sizzled.

The Greeks let go of the stake and fled to the corners of the cave.

Polyphemus pulled the spike from his eye and hurled it away from him. Blinded and groaning with pain, he fell to the floor of his cave. He bellowed for help.

All the other Cyclopes who lived on the island hurried over the dark rocks and gathered outside the cave.

"What ails you, Polyphemus?" one shouted. "Why do you break the stillness of the night with your cries? Who harms you?"

"NO ONE!" Polyphemus shouted, writhing on the floor of his cave. "No One tried to kill me! No One blinded me!"

"Well, if no one has harmed you, you must be ill," said the other Cyclopes. "And when Zeus makes one of us ill, the others can offer no help."

With no further talk, all the Cyclopes turned away and lumbered back to their own caves.

Odysseus felt laughter rise in his throat. His bold trick had worked!

Growling with rage, the giant felt along the walls with his huge hands, searching for the rock that sealed up the cave. When he found it, he pushed it away.

Odysseus was overjoyed—he and his men would soon be free! But before they could flee, the blinded Cyclops sat down in the open mouth of the cave and stretched out his huge arms. The monster grew very still. He was waiting to capture the first Greek who tried to escape.

SEVEN

THE CURSE OF THE CYCLOPS

*H*our after hour, Polyphemus waited at the mouth of the cave. Hour after hour, Odysseus wondered how he might save himself and his men. Near dawn, his gaze rested on the fat, fleecy sheep. *There* *must be a way to use them*, he thought.

Odysseus stood up silently. He quickly chose eighteen of the largest sheep. Then, using long, young willow branches, he silently bound the sheep together in groups of three. When this was done, he lashed each of his men to the belly of a middle sheep.

When all his men were concealed by the curly, white wool of the sheep, Odysseus chose the mightiest ram for himself and hid beneath it.

Dawn crept into the cave. Just as they did every morning, the sheep began to bleat and move out of the cave, heading for the mountain meadows.

As the sheep moved past the Cyclops, he ran his hands through their wool, searching for Odysseus' men. But the blind giant touched only the two outside sheep in the groups of three. Little did he imagine that the Greek warriors were hiding in the wool of the center sheep.

One by one, Odysseus' men passed smoothly and secretly past the Cyclops and out of his reach. But when the mighty ram began to move out of the cave, the giant stopped him and stroked his wool.

Odysseus held his breath as he hid beneath the ram's belly.

"Ah, my old friend," Polyphemus said to the ram, "why do you move so slowly this morning? You are always the first to run into the flowery meadow or the bubbling spring. You are always the first to come home at night. Do you move slowly now because you know your master has lost his sight? Do you grieve for me? If only you could speak and tell me where No One hides, I would catch him and bash out his brains."

The ram bleated impatiently, and the

giant let him go. The ram—and
Odysseus—moved out of the giant's
reach and beyond the cave.

As soon as they were a safe distance
away, Odysseus slipped out from beneath
the ram's belly. He quickly untied his men.
He silently urged them to hurry. Then the
men drove the giant's flock down to the
water.

The Greeks who had waited by the
ship rejoiced to see their friends alive. But
they fell to weeping when they learned of
the six who had been brutally slain.

"End your grieving now!" Odysseus

ordered. "We must put out to sea at once, before the Cyclops discovers we are gone and comes after us!"

Odysseus and his men drove the Cyclops' sheep onto their ship. Then they pushed off and rowed quickly through the calm, gray sea.

Once they were far away from shore, Odysseus stood up in the boat. "Polyphemus!" he shouted. "Polyphemus!"

In a moment, the monster appeared at the edge of the cliff. He bellowed with rage when he realized Odysseus and his men had escaped.

"You should have thought twice before making a meal of my men!" shouted Odysseus. "See how Zeus has punished you!"

The blind giant answered with a shriek of fury. He tore a slab of rock from the high cliff, and with all his might he hurled it at the Greeks.

The rock crashed into the water in front of the ship. A wave rose like a huge mountain. It scooped up the Greek ship and washed it all the way back to the Cyclopes' island and hurled it onto the beach!

Odysseus grabbed a long oar and

pushed the ship back into the water.

"Row! Row!" he shouted to his crew. "Row for your lives!"

The Greeks madly rowed their ship out to sea. As they moved far beyond the shore of the blind giant, Odysseus could not help jeering at the beast again.

"Polyphemus!" he bellowed.

His men begged Odysseus to hold his tongue. "Do not taunt the monster! He will sink our ship for certain!"

But Odysseus paid no attention to their pleas. His anger and pride were so great, he could not stop himself from making a terrible mistake: he told his true name to the giant.

"Polyphemus!" he shouted. "If anyone asks you who put out your eye, do not tell them it was No One. Tell them it was Odysseus, king of Ithaca! Odysseus, the great warrior and raider of cities! He was the one who blinded you!"

"Alas! The prophecy has come true!" boomed the giant. "Long ago, a soothsayer said a man named Odysseus would blind me. I had been waiting for someone of god-like strength. But you—you are a weakling! Come back, so I can give you a gift to prove my hospitality! To please your Zeus! So he will heal my eye!"

"Heal you?" Odysseus shouted mockingly. "Neither Zeus nor I wish to heal you, monster! I only wish to send you to the Land of the Dead!"

The giant lifted his hands and prayed to his father Poseidon, god of the seas. "Hear me, father!" he thundered. "Put a curse on Odysseus, king of Ithaca! May he never reach his home alive! If he must, may he lose his way, his ships, and all his men! May he find only sorrow and trouble on his journey!"

The Cyclops then picked up a rock even bigger than the first and hurled it at Odysseus. But this time the rock landed behind the ship, and a mountainous wave bore the Greek ship toward the goat island where the rest of the fleet waited.

Odysseus and his men were welcomed with great cries of relief. But once again joy turned to sorrow when the Greeks learned how the giant had brutally slain their friends.

As the sun went down, the Greeks feasted on mutton and wine. When night came, they lay down and slept soundly on the sand near the shore.

At dawn, Odysseus ordered his men aboard the ships. They all took their places. Then, with swift strokes, the Greeks left the goat island and headed across the rolling gray waves.

As the fleet of ships glided into the unknown, Odysseus looked about worriedly. Would the sea god Poseidon do as his monstrous son had asked? Would he punish Odysseus for blinding Polyphemus? And if so, how? And when?

EIGHT

THE PALACE OF THE
WIND GOD

Soon Odysseus and his men came upon a great rocky island. A huge bronze fortress gleamed beyond its shore. Sounds of joyful music and laughter came from within the fortress.

"Seafarers once told me about this happy kingdom," Odysseus said to his men. "It is home to Aeolus, god of the winds. He lives with his six sons and six daughters. Night and day they feast on roasted meats and listen to the music of whistles and pipes."

"But how will they receive us?" a Greek asked fearfully. Odysseus' men were still plagued with nightmarish memories of the Cyclops.

"The wind god is a friend to Zeus," said Odysseus. "I believe he will honor the gods' command that strangers must always be greeted with kindness."

Odysseus' words proved to be true. When the Greeks climbed ashore on the rocky island, Aeolus welcomed them warmly. He even invited them to stay at his palace and visit with him and his family.

Odysseus wished to be on his way as soon as possible, but he agreed to stay on Aeolus' island for a month. His men greatly needed to rest, and Odysseus had an idea of how the wind god might later help them get home.

In the following weeks, while his men

enjoyed the luxurious palace life, Odysseus told the wind god the story of the long war between the Greeks and the Trojans. He told him about the wooden horse and the fall of Troy.

Aeolus was grateful to hear such exciting tales. When Odysseus finished his stories, the god offered to give him a gift in return.

"I ask only one thing," Odysseus said. "Will you help my fleet of ships get home safely to Ithaca? Will you spare us gales and storms and give us a gentle wind to open our sails?"

Aeolus enthusiastically agreed. He called together all the winds from the east and the west, and all the winds from the north and the south. At the god's bidding, each of the winds became perfectly still. Even fierce storm winds obeyed their master's command.

Aeolus bundled all the world's winds into a sack made of oxhide, so none could hinder the Greek ships from sailing home. He left out only a gentle west wind that would carry them swiftly to Ithaca.

The wind god tied the sack of winds with a silver cord and gave the bundle to

Odysseus. Odysseus hid the sack in the hollow of his ship. He did not tell his men what was inside, for he did not want them to become lazy in their efforts to return home.

Odysseus bade farewell to the family of the wind god. Then with the help of the gentle west wind, he and his men pushed off from the rocky island.

In the days that followed, the Greek fleet kept a safe, steady course. Odysseus was so excited to be returning to his family that he could not sleep. For nine days and nights, he kept watch as the salty breeze swelled the sails of his ships.

On the tenth day, in the distance, he finally saw the wooded hills that rose from the rocky shores of Ithaca. Odysseus rejoiced. He was home! The curse of the Cyclops had come to nothing!

As the Greek ships drew closer to the island, Odysseus could see the smoke of cooking fires. Was Penelope, his beloved wife, preparing dinner for their son? The boy would be ten now, an age when he would most need a father. And were Odysseus' aging parents still alive? He prayed that they would be waiting to greet him.

The balmy west wind, the gentle waves, weariness—all soon lulled Odysseus into a deep sleep.

While he slept, some of his men began to grumble to one another.

"What is inside the sack that the wind god gave our captain?"

"I imagine it is filled with splendid gifts—gold and silver."

"Why is it only Odysseus who receives the wind god's gifts? We do all the work and receive nothing."

"Quick! Before he wakes, let us search the ship and find what he hides from us!"

And so the faithless men searched the ship and found the wind god's gift. They untied the silver threads of the ox-hide sack.

Suddenly, the mighty winds of the world rushed out and swirled into a hurricane. The storm picked up the twelve ships and sent them flying wildly over the seas, far away from the shores of Ithaca.

Odysseus leaped up from his sleep and frantically tried to change the ship's course, but it was too late. He could not fight the wild winds that his men had set free.

In great despair, Odysseus thought of hurling himself into the sea. But he clung to the mast of his ship as the winds of the storm swept his fleet back the way they had come—all the way back to the island of the wind god.

Once ashore, Odysseus ran to the god's bronze fortress. He found Aeolus feasting at the banquet table with his twelve children.

Ashamed to present himself, Odysseus stood in the back of the hall, waiting to be noticed.

One of Aeolus' sons was the first to see

him. "What has happened, Odysseus?" he called out. "Why have you returned?"

Odysseus stepped forward. He told Aeolus what his men had done. "I beg you to help us again to sail home," he said. "Will you again bundle the storm winds and give us the gentle west wind to ease our course?"

"No, Odysseus," said the wind god in a low, angry voice. "You were cursed by the Cyclops. And now, indeed, the gods punish you. We can help you no more."

Odysseus looked to the children of Aeolus, hoping to find pity. But they only stared at him in cold silence.

"Begone now!" said the wind god, "before we are punished for helping you. Leave this island at once!"

Odysseus knew the wind god spoke the truth: the curse of the Cyclops was truly upon him. The gods were punishing the Greeks for blinding Poseidon's monstrous son.

Odysseus returned to his men and ordered them to put out to sea. Ashamed of their foolish act, the men rowed valiantly. But with no wind to help, their ships drifted on the sea day after day.

As Odysseus stared at the hazy horizon, grief threatened to break his spirit. But each time he thought of Penelope and Telemachus, the fire of his determination to return to Ithaca was rekindled.

I will find my way back to my family again, he promised himself. And he leaned toward the horizon, yearning for home.

EPILOGUE

While Odysseus longed for home, his wife, Penelope, longed for his return. Over the years, news had often come to Ithaca of the fate of warriors who had been slain by the Trojans—or who had died at sea returning from the war. No word, though, had ever come to the island about the fate of Odysseus.

Most people on the island assumed that

Odysseus had died in battle or a ship-wreck. Odysseus' mother had despaired of ever seeing him again and had taken her life. In his grief and despair, Odysseus' father had withdrawn to the country and lived in seclusion.

But to everyone's amazement, Odysseus' wife held fast to the belief that her husband was still alive. Every day, as she wove cloth at her loom, she frequently glanced up, as if to catch sight of him walking in the door.

Penelope most strongly sensed Odysseus' presence when she looked upon their son, Telemachus. As the boy grew older, he reminded her more and more of his father: tall and handsome, clever and brave. The boy often asked to hear stories about Odysseus. A thousand times, he imagined his father's ship sailing over the horizon.

Penelope and Telemachus had no idea that Odysseus had been so close to them the night of the great storm. It was just as well. Sadly, neither mother nor son would lay eyes upon Odysseus for many more days, months . . . or even years to come.

ABOUT HOMER AND THE ODYSSEY

Long ago, the ancient Greeks believed that the world was ruled by a number of powerful gods and goddesses. Stories about the gods and goddesses are called the Greek myths. The myths were probably first told as a way to explain things in nature—such as weather, volcanoes, and constellations. They were also recited as entertainment.

The first written record of the Greek myths comes from a blind poet named Homer. Homer lived almost three thousand years ago. Many believe that Homer was the author of the world's two most famous epic poems: the *Iliad* and the *Odyssey*. The *Iliad* is the story of the Trojan War. The *Odyssey* tells about the long journey of Odysseus, king of an island called Ithaca. The tale concerns Odysseus' adventures on his way home from the Trojan War.

To tell his tales, Homer seems to have drawn upon a combination of his own imagination and Greek myths that had been passed down by word of mouth. A bit of actual history may have also gone into Homer's stories; there is archaeological evidence to suggest that the story of the Trojan War was based on a war fought about five hundred years before Homer's time.

Over the centuries, Homer's *Odyssey* has greatly influenced the literature of the Western world.

GODS AND GODDESSES OF ANCIENT GREECE

*T*he most powerful of all the Greek gods and goddesses was Zeus, the thunder god. Zeus ruled the heavens and the mortal world from a misty mountaintop known as Mount Olympus. The main Greek gods and goddesses were all relatives of Zeus. His brother Poseidon was ruler of the seas, and his brother Hades was ruler of the underworld. Among his many children were the gods Apollo, Mars, and Hermes, and the goddesses Aphrodite, Athena, and Artemis.

The gods and goddesses of Mount Olympus not only inhabited their mountaintop but also visited the earth, involving themselves in the daily activities of mortals such as Odysseus.

THE MAIN GODS
AND GODDESSES
AND PRONUNCIATION
OF THEIR NAMES

Zeus (zyoos), king of the gods, god of thunder

Poseidon (poh-SY-don), brother of Zeus, god of seas and rivers

Hades (HAY-deez), brother of Zeus, king of the Land of the Dead

Hera (HEE-ra), wife of Zeus, queen of the gods and goddesses

Hestia (HES-tee-ah), sister of Zeus, goddess of the hearth

Athena (ah-THEE-nah), daughter of Zeus, goddess of wisdom and war, arts and crafts

Demeter (dee-MEE-tur), goddess of crops and the harvest, mother of Persephone

Aphrodite (ah-froh-DY-tee), daughter of Zeus, goddess of love and beauty

Artemis (AR-tem-is), daughter of Zeus, goddess of the hunt

Ares (AIR-eez), son of Zeus, god of war

Apollo (ah-POL-oh), god of the sun, music, and poetry

Hermes (HUR-meez), son of Zeus, messenger god, a trickster

Hephaestus (heh-FEES-tus), son of Hera, god of the forge

Persephone (pur-SEF-oh-nee), daughter of Zeus, wife of Hades and queen of the Land of the Dead

Dionysus (dy-oh-NY-sus), god of wine and madness

PRONUNCIATION GUIDE TO OTHER PROPER NAMES

Aeolus (EE-oh-lus)

Agamemnon (ag-ah-MEM-non)

Cyclops (SY-klops)

Ithaca (ITH-ah-kah)

Odysseus (oh-DIS-yoos)

Penelope (pen-EL-oh-pee)

Polyphemus (pah-lih-FEE-mus)

Telemachus (tel-EM-ah-kus)

Trojans (TROH-junz)

A NOTE ON THE SOURCES

$\mathcal{T}$he story of the *Odyssey* was originally written down in the ancient Greek language. Since that time there have been countless translations of Homer's story into other languages. I consulted a number of English translations, including those written by Alexander Pope, Samuel Butler, Andrew Lang, W. H. D. Rouse,

Edith Hamilton, Robert Fitzgerald, Allen Mandelbaum, and Robert Fagles.

Homer's *Odyssey* is divided into twenty-four books. The first volume of *Tales from the Odyssey* is derived from books nine and ten of Homer's *Odyssey*.

The story concerning Odysseus' recruitment for the Trojan War originated with the second-century A.D. writer Hyginus. The account of the Trojan horse is derived from Virgil's *Aeneid*. Apollodorus' account of the fall of Troy mentions that the name of Athena was inscribed on the wooden horse.

ABOUT THE AUTHOR

MARY POPE OSBORNE is the author of the best selling Magic Tree House series. She has also written many acclaimed historical novels and retellings of myths and folktales, including *Kate and the Beanstalk* and *New York's Bravest*. She lives with her husband in New York City and Connecticut.

Zeus

Hera

Artemis

Hephaestus

Ares

Apollo

Athena

GODS *and* GODDESSES
of ANCIENT GREECE

Hermes

Dionysus

Aphrodite

Hestia

Demeter

Persephone

Poseidon

Hades